# The Shadow in the Pond

### by RON ROY

*Cover illustration by Gil Cohen*

## SCHOLASTIC BOOK SERVICES

NEW YORK • TORONTO • LONDON • AUCKLAND • SYDNEY • TOKYO

ISBN 0-590-31304-5

12 11 10 9 8 7 6 5 4 3 2 1          10          0 1 2 3 4 5/8
                    Printed in the U.S.A.                    11

*for David McLean, who saw the Shadow*

## ...1

"But why can't I, Dad?" Nick pleaded. "All the kids in the city are taking SCUBA lessons this summer. And it wouldn't cost me half as much out here now that we have our own pond where I could practice."

"No!" His father gave his newspaper a shake for emphasis. "And, Nick, I don't want you poking around the bottom of that pond — if the pond *has* a bottom — with or without scuba gear. There's no telling what's down there."

"But, Dad, I'd be —"

"No, Nick, and that's final!" After a pause his father added in a calmer voice, "When you're older, perhaps we'll see about scuba lessons. Maybe in Hartford, at a regular pool. But for now, they're out, and so is the pond."

"Even for swimming?" Nick sounded really shocked.

"Even for swimming — at least, until we know more about the place."

"Oh boy," Nick sighed. This was too much. He got up and went out to the porch to think. Of course, he should have known. Anytime he wanted to try something new, it ended like this. "No, you can't." Or, "Wait till you're older." Especially when the subject was diving. What was there about swimming underwater that bugged his father so? And how was he ever to become an underwater explorer if he couldn't even swim in their backyard pond?

Left alone, Nick's father put aside the paper and rubbed his eyes wearily. He could never make Nick understand how he felt. And now there was this stupid pond that had come with the farm. But how could he tell his son that water terrified him?

Mason's fear went way back, to the summer at his uncle's lake when he was six, just learning to dog-paddle. One afternoon, when they were all down at the dock, his uncle had suddenly picked him up and dropped him in, way over his head. Barry Mason never forgot the panic he felt as he struggled in that cold, dark water. He still had nightmares about it.

If it hadn't been for their mother, Nick and Gwen might never have learned to swim. She had insisted that they take lessons in the city. And she had made their father promise to let Nick take scuba lessons when he was fifteen.

Nick thought about that now as he sat on the porch steps. His fifteenth birthday was one year and thirty-seven days away. To Nick it seemed forever, especially now that they owned a real pond. What a laugh! The pond had been the only thing that had made the move from New York City to Connecticut worthwhile to him.

His mother had promised to get him a mask and flippers for his fourteenth birthday. He'd bet that Dad wouldn't let her. Anyway, he intended to practice diving in the pond, with or without permission.

## ••• 2

No one in Glastonbury, Connecticut, knew why the pond behind the Masons' house was called Shadow Pond, since it lay in the sun, away from the woods and big shade trees. Old Mr. McKinley had named it; he had owned the pond and the land around it longer than anyone could recall. And until the day he died, "mean old McKinley" chased kids away whenever he saw them trying to sneak a swim in the pond.

Fred Hurlburt, who taught science at the high school, told his students that the pond had been scraped out by a glacier a million years ago. The hole had filled up gradually with rains and underground springs. Nobody knew how deep it was. But Fred said that most glacier holes were very deep.

The kids around there fished at Shadow Pond now and then, but they never caught a fish of any size. Some people said all the fish were at the bottom and that's why you couldn't catch them. But others said that was crazy. Falls River Pond, about ten miles away, was also a deep glacier hole. And it was full of large mouth bass and pickerel. They said the reason no one caught anything at Shadow Pond was that it had been fished out, long ago.

No one had ever bothered to ask old man McKinley why he called his waterhole Shadow Pond. Or why he chased the kids away, or why there were no fish. And that was too bad. Because the old man had known the answers from his boyhood, when he had first seen the Shadow.

When Mr. McKinley died at eighty-three, the farm was put up for sale. That was how the Masons saw the ad in *The New York Times*.

The real estate agent who showed them the place was Mary Hurlburt, Fred's wife. Her boys had been chased away from McKinley's pond as often as they had sneaked through his orchard with towels draped around their necks. Usually when that happened, they'd ask their mother to drive them over to Falls River Pond. On the way, they'd laugh and tell her how "mean old McKinley" had come shuffling out of the barn to yell at them. Bart, the oldest, would hunch his back over and shake his fist, imitating the old man's voice: "You boys go t'bottom o' this here pond, you'll not come up alive. Now take yer skinny selves right offa this propity and don't come back, you hear?"

Mary Hurlburt used to laugh at these stories, but sometimes she wondered. In a strange way, she was glad the old man had chased her sons away. Thank Heaven they were grown now and she didn't have to think about it. That is, not until she was handed the job of selling the farm — and the pond — to other families.

Most of the people to whom she showed the farm loved the idea of having their own pond. But Mary was always a little surprised at herself, the way she turned their questions aside. She never really lied; she just never mentioned the feeling she had that something wasn't quite right about Shadow Pond.

So when Barry Mason inquired rather anxiously if the pond was deep, Mary Hurlburt answered, "It doesn't appear to be, does it?" And when Olivia Mason asked how the pond had got its name, she said, "Perhaps there were trees here once." Then she walked away, saying, "Come, I must show you this wonderful old barn." And, patting four-year-old Ann Mason on the head, said, "Why, there's even a stall for a pony."

They'd all trooped off to see the barn and what was left of the peach orchard. If they had turned back for another look at the pond, they would have seen the wiggly water trail of a muskrat carrying a branch to its nest. And they would have seen a shadow rise behind the swimming muskrat...and the small waves that were left when it was dragged to the bottom of Shadow Pond.

Barry Mason gave Mrs. Hurlburt a check as down payment for the purchase of the farm. And as they drove back to New York City, the family discussed all the advantages of their "new" house.

The parents were thrilled about owning a genuine old farmhouse and all the land that went with it. Mr. Mason was going to set up a workshop in the barn. His wife said she couldn't wait to start a vegetable garden. And the youngest, Ann, bounced around, chattering about "my puppy." Her parents had told her she could have one, now that they had space for a dog.

Nick and his sister Gwen knew they'd miss all their friends in the city. But Gwen was too happy about having a room of her own at last to think about that. Nick, of course, had been won over by the pond. He looked forward to a summer of swimming, never dreaming that his father was going to declare it out of bounds.

## ••• 3

Munch Ralston was lying in a hammock on his porch, eating chocolate chip cookies, the day the Masons moved in next door. It was eighty-eight degrees in the shade and Munch was enjoying his three favorite pastimes: lying in his hammock, eating chocolate chip cookies, and watching other people work.

He counted the cookies left in the bag. There were only three. His mother would have a lot to say if she found out he had gone off his diet again. She never seemed to realize he was never really on it.

Hoping she might forget she had ever bought the cookies, Munch made a cookie sandwich (two cookies on the outside, one in the middle), jammed the

8

whole thing into his mouth, crumpled the bag, and stuffed it in his pocket.

"GOTCHA!"

Gwen Mason, seeing the boy lying in his hammock, had climbed over the stone wall separating their properties to introduce herself. And of course she had her camera with her, so she snapped Munch just as his mouth snapped shut.

"I've never seen anyone eat three cookies at one time," she marveled to Munch, who was trying to heave his one hundred sixty-two pounds out of the hammock.

"I do it all the time," he answered. "I'm Munch Ralston. Who are you?"

"My real name is Gwendolyn Carolyn Mason. But my brother—that's him over there with the globe on his head—calls me Goon. You may call me Gwen." She looked at the empty hammock. "Mind if I try it?"

Munch waved her into the hammock and lowered himself onto the edge of the porch. He continued to watch the movers.

"How old are you?" he asked, more to take his mind off the ice cream in the refrigerator than to learn the age of this skinny camera bug.

"Eleven, but I'll be twelve next April. I'm a Taurus."

"You're a *what*?"

"A Taurus, you know, my sign. I'm a bull. What are you?"

"That's easy, I'm a pig." Munch thought this was about the funniest thing he had ever said. He rolled over on the porch, laughing like a madman.

"Why do you make fun of yourself?" Gwen asked him curiously, when he had calmed down.

"Why do you sneak up on people and snap pictures when they're deep in thought?"

"It looked to me like you were deep in cookies. But to answer your question, I have to practice taking pictures of people who don't know I'm doing it. I'm going to be a famous photographer and take pictures of celebrities. My brother, Nick, is going to be an underwater explorer like that French guy. What are you going to be?"

"What do you mean?" Munch Ralston had never thought about anything as active as a career. These days he could work up a sweat just going to the mailbox at the end of the driveway. He found it hard to believe that anyone would deliberately plan to grow up and get a job.

Then he smiled. "Maybe I'll be a bird-watcher. That way I can work in my hammock."

Munch was starting to chuckle again. Before he could launch himself into another laughing fit, Gwen leaped out of the hammock and started to walk away. "Come and see our puppy. We got him for Annie; he's half collie." Munch followed her and struggled to climb over the stone wall that Gwen vaulted like an Olympic trainee.

"Who's Annie and who's half collie?"

"Ann is my little sister. And this," Gwen said, grabbing a wiggly ball of fur, "is Bingo. Want to hold him?"

By now Munch had negotiated the wall and caught up with Gwen. He was standing, trying to get his breath, when she thrust the puppy into his arms.

"Get it away!" he screamed. "I'm allergic!"

Nick and his mother were busy carrying small things into the house. When they heard the scream, they turned in time to see Gwen, holding Bingo at arms' length, running after a very fat boy.

"I see that Goon girl is making herself popular with the neighbors already," said Nick. "How come *she* isn't working?"

"Gwen," called his mother, "there's still a lot left to do. Please help. You can visit later."

Gwen came back slowly. She made a face at her brother. She was pretty sure he had said something to their mother about her goofing off.

# •••4

Two weeks later the Masons were settled in their new old house. Bingo, a fast-growing puppy, had adopted the back porch as his napping place, and the Masons had put his basket there. Today he lay there as usual, dozing while he waited for the children to show up. It was shady and cool in the early part of the day. But in the afternoon, the summer sun shone full on him, and he woke up, hot and thirsty.

He went over to his water bowl but it was empty. Then he ran to the back door and whined, but nobody came. Suddenly he remembered the pond. With a leap he was off the porch and racing around the barn. He stood at the water's edge, trying to lean over to drink, but his front feet slipped and he tumbled into the pond with a splash. Once in, he was surprised to find out he could swim. He paddled around happily in the cool water, making ripples that fanned out across the pond.

Olivia Mason was weeding her new garden, trying not to disturb the little seedlings. Suddenly she heard a high, frantic yipping.

"That sounds as if Bingo is in trouble," she told herself, getting up. The cries seemed to come from the direction of the barn. Mrs. Mason stepped inside and called, "Bingo? Here, pup!" Nothing stirred in there. Then she looked on either side of the barn, but saw no sign of the little dog. By now, the frantic yipping had ended in an odd splashing sound.

"He may have gotten stung by a bee," she thought, "and dove in the pond to cool off." Then she went back to her weeding, got absorbed in her plans for the garden, and forgot all about Bingo.

Later, she went in to get dinner ready, still thinking about the garden. Her family had laughed when she insisted on putting one in so late in June. Most gardens had been growing for over a month. But she went right on planting seeds, and now, two weeks later, there were tiny radishes forming, and the beginnings of lettuce heads. It was very satisfying. Mrs. Mason smiled, thinking how happy they all were in this lovely place.

Ann cried when Bingo did not show up for his supper. Her mother suddenly remembered what she'd heard earlier that day, and promised Ann they would go looking for her pet right after dinner.

To comfort her sister, Gwen said, "He probably made friends with another dog and followed him home. He'll come back when he gets hungry."

"He may have chased a rabbit and gone so far away he got lost. We'll find him," promised Nick.

After dinner, Nick and his father went looking in various directions, calling Bingo. But there was no answering yip, no sign of the little pup. Once, when they passed the pond, Mason asked his son, "He couldn't have fallen in and drowned, could he?"

"No, Dad." Nick was very positive. "All dogs, even puppies, swim the minute they're in the water. They love it."

"Hmm," answered his father. He wished again that the pond wasn't here, so close to the house.

Ann cried herself to sleep that night. Her mother couldn't seem to comfort her. Later, as she closed the child's bedroom door softly, she felt a sudden sadness. She knew, somehow, that Bingo would not be back. But it was hard to believe that any dog, even a puppy, could drown by himself. Perhaps, after all, she had imagined that splashing sound. Perhaps Bingo had found another home.

# ... 5

Nick sat on the porch steps and stared across the yard at the garden, then the barn, and finally, the pond. Beyond that, the woods went clear to the hills until mountains and sky met in a hazy blur. His mother and father loved this sight. But he felt like a prisoner, locked in by the empty view.

Right now, he'd give anything to be back in New York City, where everything he wanted was close to their apartment. He could walk to his friends' homes, or to the pet store, or the library, or the "Y," or even to Central Park, when the gang felt like playing ball.

Why did his parents have to go and buy this dumb place in the country, where he couldn't even swim in his own pond? "We can feel safe here," they'd said. Well, he couldn't take scuba lessons because it wasn't safe. He couldn't ride his bike to town because the traffic was dangerous. And there was only one kid his age, a lazy, scared kid at that, instead of the gang he used to fool around with in the city. He was bored, bored and fed up, and sick and tired of just hanging around with nothing to do.

Before Nick realized what he was doing, he had walked into the garage, hopped on his bike, and was moving down the road. He thought briefly of asking Munch to ride to town with him, and quickly decided against it. Not after what happened the last time they had gone biking together.

He and Munch had gone to the quarry to fool around on the bulldozers that were left out all night. That, too, was off limits for Nick, so when they noticed it was getting late, they jumped on their bikes and tore out of there. "Tore" was the right word. Nick's front tire had hit a rock, spilling him into a ditch. He had broken a spoke on his wheel and put a gash in his knee.

Munch had to promise not to mention where they'd been to anyone. "It's my sister," Nick explained. "I told you I'm not supposed to go to the quarry and fool around with the equipment. If Goon girl finds out, she'll blab to my parents and I'll be grounded."

Munch had agreed to stay mum, but Nick had an uneasy feeling. Gwen seemed to smell out trouble when her brother was in it.

Sure enough, Nick spent the next day sitting in his room, grounded.

Gwen had seen him hide his bike in Munch's garage and then sneak upstairs to his room with a bloody knee. She'd decided to do some detective work on Munch.

First, she offered him cookies, but he had his own sources. Then she tried to bribe him with money, but he got a big allowance. So she had no choice but to threaten to tell his mother he was cheating on his diet again. (By chance, Gwen had stumbled on a box of food, and the rope Munch used to pull it up to his room. It was while she was trying to catch a garter snake that had slithered into the bushes under Munch's window. The snake got away but when Gwen saw the box and the rope, she knew she had Munch in the palm of her hand.)

When confronted, Munch choked, then told all — how they had gone to the quarry and Nick had hurt himself. Gwen did keep her promise not to tell Munch's mother on him. But she crossed her fingers as she promised Munch she'd keep the boys' trip a secret.

That night at dinner Gwen felt both mean and pleased, watching her brother try to explain how he had damaged his bike and his knee at the quarry. (Gwen tried to keep in mind the times that Nick had blabbed to their parents about *her*.)

Their father listened politely to Nick's explanation,

then invited him to spend the next day in his room. Thinking.

So that was why Nick decided not to invite Munch today. Munch could be gotten at too easily.

Seventeen minutes from the time Nick left the house, he was chaining his bike to a fire hydrant on the main street of Glastonbury. First he stopped at Frosty's for a reviving coke, then he pedaled through the traffic around town.

When he saw the sign in the window he almost drove his bike into the store. He got off and read it again, to make sure.

**DAVE'S DIVING DEN**

is going out of business soon!

**ALL EQUIPMENT HALF PRICE**

But it was the display behind the sign that made Nick's mouth water. Hanging all over some manikins which looked a little like dead bodies, were masks, snorkels, fins, tanks, wet suits—everything a scuba diver would ever need.

## •••6

Jangling bells announced Nick as he entered the store. Dave Jones jumped up from the cot where he had been napping. He ran his fingers through his hair and stepped through the strings of beads that separated the shop from his living quarters.

"Help you?" Dave sized up the kid through sleepy eyes. About fourteen years old, family has a little dough, wants to learn to dive.

"C-can I look at your tanks? The ones that are on s-sale, like the sign says." Nick had practiced lowering his voice so he'd sound older. It didn't work. He sounded like Gwen with a cold.

Dave almost smiled at his young customer, but he didn't. He hadn't really felt like smiling since his store had started losing money.

"How much do you plan to spend?" he asked.

"I don't exactly have the money with me," Nick managed to say. "I'm really just looking. Uh — how much do they cost?"

"Fifty and up for the new ones." Dave saw the boy turn pale, and added, "But you're lucky. I got a used one in the back. Want to see it?"

"Yes, th-thank you," Nick stammered. Why was he so nervous? he wondered.

"Come on back here." Dave pushed aside the beaded curtain and Nick walked into a dark, stale-smelling room.

"Excuse the mess." Dave kicked a boot out of the way and turned on a light. Nick saw what he meant. The small room contained an unmade bed and a bureau piled with overflowing ash trays, unwashed dishes, and empty cans.

"I only got this one used tank left, but it's in real good shape." Dave pulled a box out from under the bed. "Let you have it for twenty. Interested?"

Nick thought fast. He could probably get that much in loans from his sister and Moneybags Munch. Plus his own allowance. "I'll have to come back when I have the money. Can you, I mean, will that be all right?"

Dave knew he could sell the tank if he could get a deposit. "You got any money on you now?"

Nick dug into his jeans and came up with two

crumpled bills and some change. "Two dollars and eighteen cents, but I'll get the rest by tomorrow. You won't sell it, will you?"

"No, I won't sell it, kid," Dave answered. This time he did smile.

## ••• 7

Olivia Mason made sure that Ann was asleep before she lay down in her own stifling room. The windows were wide open but there was no breeze, and the pillow was hot under her head. A heat wave had blanketed the East for over a week. Even in the country, the days were blistering and at night the bedrooms stayed hot. Nobody in the Mason family was getting much sleep.

Nick and Gwen couldn't understand why they didn't have air-conditioning here as they'd had in New York. Barry Mason tried to explain that in the country you didn't usually need air-conditioning.

After this heat wave passed they'd be fine, he'd promised.

And they really would be, Mrs. Mason thought now, as she lay in her hot bedroom wishing for a breeze.

Ann had been put down for her nap wearing just her shorts. Her room had only one window; it was wide open, but she was perspiring and her blond hair was plastered to her forehead.

Suddenly she sat up, crying. She had been having a bad dream. Something had been chasing her, and was about to wrap its hairy arms around her, when she awoke. Squeezed in her arms was her new stuffed dog, Bingo, named after the puppy that never came home. The toy did look a little like Bingo, and Ann talked to it as if it could really hear and understand her.

Now she held the toy dog by its left ear as she pushed open the door of her parents' bedroom.

"Mommy, I'm thirsty," she said as she approached the bed.

Her mother dimly heard her. She felt drugged with the heat. "Ask Gwennie or Nick, O.K., Honey? Mommy's tired." Ann left her mother and went down the stairs, her puppy bump-bumping behind her as she dragged it by one ear.

Gwen and her brother weren't around. Ann was alone downstairs. She pushed a chair up to the sink in the kitchen to get a drink of water. But her short arms couldn't reach the faucet, so she got down and opened the refrigerator. She took out a quart of milk, had her drink, and then went into the backyard.

The day was at its hottest. The little girl shielded her eyes from the glaring sun as she looked around for someone to play with. But the yard was empty. Where were Nick and Gwennie? she wondered. Maybe they were hiding again. Sometimes, when they wanted to go off by themselves, they'd hide until she gave up. But today Ann wasn't giving up. She really wanted to find them.

She ran to the barn and peered into the cool darkness. She was afraid to go in and search. There were spiders in the dim corners. Then she thought of another hiding place. Laughing and dragging Bingo behind her, Ann went to look for her brother and sister in the tall weeds at the edge of the pond.

Mrs. Mason sat up suddenly. Something had awakened her. But what? She sat listening a moment, then she realized how completely still it was. Peaceful. She smiled and lay back, thinking of the contrast between this place and the noisy city.

How happy they all were in their "new" old house. Nicky and Gwen had that nice fat boy next door to play with, and Ann didn't seem to mind not having anyone her age around.

Ann! Where was she? Ann had come into the bedroom for some reason and she had sent her to look for Gwen and Nick. Where were they all? Mrs. Mason got up quickly, patted her hair, and hurried downstairs.

Ann sat on a flat stone at the edge of the pond, paddling her feet in the water. Gwennie and Nick were not hiding in the bushes after all, but now she didn't care. She could play in the water all she wanted; there was nobody around to say "No, Ann" to her.

She decided to teach her new puppy to drink from the pond. Only the bad puppy wouldn't even try. She put his mouth in the water again and again, but he wouldn't stick out his tongue to lap. Ann was too busy to notice that each time she dunked her toy into the pond, a shadow moved closer.

The thing on the bottom of the pond had not eaten for a week, and the smallest ripple on the pond's surface could bring it up from the bottom. Now it stopped, waited. Cold, unblinking eyes tried to focus. There was something moving slowly, in and out. Claws gripping the bottom, an inch at a time, the Shadow moved toward its meal.

Downstairs, Mrs. Mason could not find any of her children. Nicky and Gwen must have taken their little sister for a walk, she thought. Or maybe they were all next door at the Ralstons'. She would give Joan Ralston a call if they didn't show up soon.

But when she saw the chair at the sink and the milk still on the counter, Mrs. Mason knew that Ann had left the house alone. She called, but no one answered. In a panic, she rushed out the back door, letting it slam. It was just as she was running toward the barn that she heard the screams.

## ●●●8

Gwen had been bored on that hot July day. Her brother and Munch were off somewhere, and of course they wouldn't think of inviting her to come with them. Bingo had run away over a week ago so she couldn't play with him; even Annie and her mother were napping.

That was how Gwen happened to wander into Nick's room, and to be poking in his things. Maybe she could find out why he had needed to borrow almost all her savings a few days ago. He had come to her, all out of breath, and asked how much money she had in her peanut butter jar.

"Oh, I don't know. Some sum, I guess." Gwen Mason knew to the penny how much she had in the jar. Twelve dollars and seventy-three cents. But she didn't intend to tell old stingy. The last time he had borrowed money, it had taken him almost six months to pay it back.

"What do you want to know for?" she'd asked.

"Just something. Come on, Gwennie, how much you got? I'll pay you back, honest."

In the end she had given him ten dollars, on the condition that he would pay it back out of his allowance at fifty cents a week. Nick agreed, slapped her jovially on the back, and rushed out, then poked his head back into the room. "Uh, Gwen," he'd said, "promise you won't tell Mom and Dad. O.K.?"

"Why not?" Gwen thought he was going to let her in on the secret.

"Because then they'll know I'm buying them an anniversary present, Goonie-bird. Promise not to tell?"

Gwen smiled at her big brother. "O.K., I promise. Buy them something nice."

"Thanks, Sis, you're great. I will, I'll buy them something they'll really like. See you around."

Gwen had put the peanut butter jar back in her closet behind her blue suitcase. Then she'd stood by her window and watched Nick hurdle the stone wall and run over to Munch's. She'd wondered how long it would take to get Munch to tell her what the money was really for. Her parents' anniversary had been three months ago.

But Gwen was disappointed, because Munch wouldn't talk. He had found a new hiding place for his after-dinner snack, so she couldn't threaten to tell his mother about the box under the window. Finally she had stomped off the porch leaving Munch lying in his hammock.

Munch had been thinking about Nick's promise. "If you lend me eight dollars, we'll be partners. How about it?"

"Partners in what?" Munch had asked. He didn't really care, though. He'd walk a tight-rope blindfolded to be Nick's friend.

"You'll see if you let me have the money. Come on, are you going to let me have eight bucks or not?" So Munch had handed over the sock filled with quarters he'd been saving for ten months, out of his allowance. Also, he'd had to swear on all the Bibles in the world not to say anything to Gwen.

"If she finds out, the partnership is off," Nick had said as he stuffed the sock into his jeans. They both remembered the quarry incident.

That had been three days ago. Now Gwen stood in her brother's room, looking for a clue. Nothing. His bed looked as if it had been made by rats playing tug-of-war with his blankets.

She looked under it and saw dust and dirty socks. His closet held more of the same, plus his comics collection, tennis racket, and fishing pole. But no clues.

She decided to borrow the fishing pole and try her luck at the pond. The hook dangling from the string was big enough to catch one of the sharks that grinned down at her from the posters decorating Nick's walls.

On her way to the pond, she turned over a few rocks to try to find a worm, but she gave up after six centipedes, three crickets, and about a million spiders. Yuck. At the edge of the pond she caught a small frog, but she didn't put him on the hook as she had seen her brother do. (The idea was to put the hook through the back leg so it could still swim.)

She removed the hook and tied the string around the frog's back leg. She knew she wouldn't catch anything without a hook, but it would be fun to watch the frog swim around.

She put him in the water and watched as he took off for the middle of the pond. Then she reeled him in and let him swim out again. The last time she reeled in she thought she saw a movement, under the water. But before she could toss the frog out again, she saw her brother and Munch. They were coming toward the pond.

She hid the pole in the bushes at the edge of the pond, sat down on a big rock, closed her eyes, and pretended to be sunbathing. She sat still, waiting for the boys to see her. When nothing happened, she opened her eyes just a little.

Nick and Munch were going away from the pond, toward the woods. She got quietly to her feet, and, crouching low, began to follow. Since her camera was around her neck, she didn't forget it. But the pole stayed where it was, one end in the bushes, the other near the water. The frog, with only six inches of string for freedom, was trapped. At first he hopped in and out of the water, struggling to get loose. Finally he gave up, closed his eyes, sat in the water, and was warmed by the July sun.

Following the boys through the woods proved to be as easy as falling off a log (which she did, several times). Then she saw that they were headed toward a small cabin. She waited, and when they went inside, she tiptoed up and peeked through the window. Holding back a giggle, she snapped a picture of what she saw there.

On her way home again, she laughed out loud. She knew what Nick had done with the money, and she had a picture to prove it. There were two more pictures left on the roll. She took one of a curious squirrel, and decided to save the last. She wanted a picture of the little frog before she took the string off his leg and let him go.

But the frog was already gone, and so was the pole. Funny, she had left it right here, hadn't she? How could it just disappear? Maybe Mom had seen it and carried it back to the house. Gwen hurried away from the pond, hoping to get the pole back to her brother's room before he found out she had taken it.

## ●●●9

Three days ago, after Nick borrowed money from Gwen, he wondered if it was a good idea asking Munch to be his partner. But he needed the eight dollars. Besides, Munch might come in handy, later.

Dave Jones had kept his word about holding the tank, and when Nick went back the next day with the money, it was waiting for him. Dave had even shined it up and filled it with oxygen. He was a nice guy.

When he asked Nick how many times he'd dived, Nick didn't mean to lie. But he thought there might be some kind of law about selling a diving tank to someone who had never dived before. So he made up a story about this uncle in California who used to take him diving all the time. Dave seemed to believe him.

"Just remember, never go down alone, and always wear a diving watch. You don't want to be down there when the oxygen gives out."

Nick didn't have a diving watch. In fact, he didn't even have a regular watch, but he knew someone who did. Now he was glad he had made Munch his partner. From his books he knew how to work the oxygen valve and about the little window that showed how much was left.

Dave showed him how to hold the mouthpiece and how to adjust the back straps. He didn't mention the little leak in the hose that went from the tank to the mouthpiece. It was only a small leak, and besides, the kid could look at the dial, couldn't he? If he checked his watch and remembered the dial, he wouldn't have any problems.

When Nick left the shop, Dave watched him through the window as he strapped the tank to his bike. Nice kid, he thought. Maybe I should have offered a few lessons. Dave didn't believe the story about the uncle in California. Something about the kid's eyes when he said it.

Nick rode home on his bike, but in his mind's eye he was already on the bottom of Shadow Pond.

These pleasant daydreams were suddenly interrupted by a thought that had been nagging him from the time he'd first seen the tank. Where was he going to hide it? Not in his room, with his sister spying around. Munch's house? No, Munch's mother might get curious.

Then he thought of the cabin. Perfect! He had discovered it one day while exploring the woods behind their house. He was pretty sure no one ever went there, from the look of the place, and he could sneak away from home whenever he wanted.

So he had stowed the precious tank in the cabin as soon as he got back from Dave Jones's store. For once, Gwen hadn't seen him.

Now Nick was keeping his promise to Munch by taking him to see what his eight dollars had helped to buy. As they passed by the pond Nick saw his sister sitting in the sun by the water. He jabbed Munch in the side and put his finger to his lips. He sure didn't want her to follow him today, of all days.

"That was close," Munch whispered when they had gone farther. "Think she heard us?"

"I doubt it," Nick answered, grinning. "She's too busy getting a tan. Besides, Mom likes her to stick around while she's resting, in case Ann wakes up."

Munch opened the bag he was carrying. He stuffed half a tuna sandwich into his mouth and offered the other half to Nick. "Thanks. Hey, is that watch waterproof?"

"I don't think so. My mother makes me take it off

whenever I take a shower. Why?"

Nick slipped the watch off Munch's wrist and turned it over. "Says here it's shock-proof, dust-proof, and tarnish-proof. Must be waterproof too, I'll bet."

"But what do you want with a waterproof watch?"

"You'll see in about two minutes." At the end of that time they came into the little clearing where the cabin stood, or leaned. Munch was out of breath from the walk and plopped himself down on the doorsill.

"You paid twenty dollars for this shack?" Munch couldn't believe that his hard-earned savings went for a few boards stuck together with cobwebs. "It isn't even worth twenty cents!"

"No, Dumbo, not this dump. This is just where I'm hiding it till I get to use it. Come on, let's go in."

Nick pushed the door open and found the tank where he had left it, hidden under an old mattress in the corner. "Well, what do you think?" he asked Munch.

"Holy baloney," Munch whistled. "Where'd you ever get it?"

Nick told Munch about the books he'd been reading, about Dave's store, and about how he planned to explore the bottom of the pond.

"But what're your folks going to say?" Munch asked. "Will they let you?"

"Help me get this thing on," Nick said, slinging

the tank over his back. "And they're not going to say anything, because they're not going to know about it. Nobody's going to know about it, especially my sister. Right, Munch, old pal?"

If it hadn't been for the spider that chose to drop between them at that minute, Munch would not have yelled, Nick would not have laughed, and maybe they would have noticed the face at the window. Or heard the click of the camera.

## ...10

When Mrs. Mason heard the child's screams, she froze. "Ann, Annie, where are you?" She started toward the barn, almost hysterical with fright, then rushed toward the back of the property. As she went around the corner of the barn, Ann came running toward her, arms outstretched, terror on her face. Mrs. Mason dropped to her knees and grabbed her daughter and held her close. "Oh, Baby," she crooned. "What happened?"

Gwen had been back from the pond for awhile, and was checking her brother's room to see if anyone had returned the fishing rod, when she heard the screams. She rushed down into the yard in time to see her mother carrying Ann toward the house. Ann was sobbing wildly. Her mother was still trying to get the child to tell her what had happened.

But Ann was too scared to talk. All she did was whimper and cling tightly, her arms almost strangling her mother. They talked soothingly to her, and finally Ann let them put her gently down on her bed. Gwen stayed with her while Mrs. Mason telephoned her husband at the office.

Gwen looked around for a toy or doll that might comfort Ann. "Where's your puppy, Annie? Do you want Gwen to get Bingo for you?" But at the word "Bingo" the bawling started all over again, and when their mother came back she found Gwen once again trying to soothe her little sister.

"I just asked if she wanted her p-u-p-p-y and she started to holler all over again," Gwen told her mother. "It's funny, Bingo doesn't seem to be in the room. Annie takes it everywhere. Maybe she lost it."

When Ann felt better, Gwen took her downstairs for milk and cookies. Mrs. Mason searched Ann's room, but she couldn't find the toy dog either.

As she went downstairs, she was thinking of the phone conversation she'd had with Barry a few minutes ago.

"What do you mean she was at the pond alone?" he demanded.

"Well, I know that Ann understands she's not to go near the pond unless someone is with her, but, Barry, the child was sobbing and so frightened, I didn't have the heart to scold her.

"I was taking a rest, and told her to look for Gwen or Nick, but they were off who knows where. Ann must have gone out to look for them."

"Well, I'll have a little talk with those two. I don't want Ann near that pond alone, ever."

Before he hung up, Barry Mason promised to try and get home a little earlier than usual, and his wife went off to find the girls. Her head had begun to ache again. It was the worry, probably.

The children were all on the Ralstons' porch. Hearing Ann's happy squeals as the older ones pushed her in the hammock, her mother found it hard to remember the child's frightened sobs of a little while ago. Barry had said that maybe a snake or bullfrog had scared her. The thought of a snake made Mrs. Mason shudder. Were there any poisonous ones around here? She'd have to ask Fred Hurlburt about that.

Gwen looked up and saw her mother standing by the stone wall. She was motioning for Gwen to come home, and Gwen quickly joined her.

"I didn't want to say anything in front of Annie, but she may have left the toy down by the pond. Would you have a look? I want to start supper because Daddy's coming home early."

"Should I give it to her as soon as I find it?"

"No. Just stick it in her room as if nothing had happened. She's probably forgotten all about what scared her, anyway."

Her mother took Ann home, and the boys went up to Munch's room to play his hockey game. Gwen walked down to the pond. She walked all around it, but saw no sign of Ann's stuffed dog. Then something caught her eye. There, under a foot of water, was Nick's fishing pole. She had to reach in to her elbow to get it.

"How did it get in the water?" she puzzled. She knew she had left it on the bank. Imagining her brother's anger if he found out, she dried the reel carefully on her shorts.

The handle still turned and the sun had dried everything else by the time she reached the house. Maybe she'd just stick it back in his closet. Wait a minute: what had happened to the frog that was tied to the string? In her hurry to follow the boys she'd forgotten all about it.

There was no frog on the string now, and no knot either. And how did the pole get in the water? Could that little frog have dragged it in? Gwen doubted it. But something, or someone, had thrown in or pulled in the pole. Who? Or what?

# ••• 11

Mr. Mason waited till Ann was in bed before he questioned the family about what had happened that afternoon. His wife once again told how she had come down to the kitchen and found the milk on the counter. Just before the screams.

"But why was a four-year-old left alone to get her own drink? And to wander off to get into who knows what kind of trouble?" Now he was staring at Gwen. "Well?"

Gwen didn't want to say that she had been at the pond earlier and had spied on her brother. So she just said she had gone for a walk.

Then it was Nick's turn. He couldn't very well say he had been showing Munch the tank, so he muttered that he'd been with Munch in the woods.

"All right, but from now on there is to be someone looking out for Ann every minute — with that miserable pond out back. I don't want to think of what might have happened. Or what it was that scared Ann half to death."

When dinner was finally over, Gwen excused herself and went to her room. Seeing the camera, she decided to take the film out and mail it to that photo place in Hartford. Her mother could pick up the pictures when she went shopping. But then Gwen remembered she had one more frame left. Maybe she'd go into her mother's room and get some stuff to dress up in, and have her brother take her picture.

She went to find Nick, and when he wasn't in his room she looked to see if the fishing pole was where she had left it. It was. Maybe he hadn't even noticed that it had been touched.

Then she saw the note on his desk. It was definitely in his disgusting handwriting, so she decided to read it:

Munchy,

Here's the sizes of the wood we need. See if you can get any from your garage and I'll try mine. And we need

hamer, nales and a big saw. No blab-
bing to you know who.

Your pal,

Nick Mason

Then there were some numbers and a drawing of
something that looked like a lot of pieces of wood tied
together. Gwen smiled, and snapped a picture of
herself looking in her brother's mirror snapping a
picture of herself. Then she picked up the note and
walked out of the room. When Nick realized it was
missing he'd come running to her. Which was exactly
what she wanted him to do.

Right now Nick Mason was thinking of other
things. After his father's lecture he went outside for a
walk. It was still light enough, so he decided to walk
down by the pond to look for bullfrogs. The water
looked so peaceful that Nick was tempted to go for a
swim. But he knew his father would have a fit if he
returned with wet hair.

Instead, he looked around for some smooth stones
to skip across the water. He found one that was perfect, and it made seven hops before it finally sank out
of sight. That was when he saw it, floating mostly
under water, with just the nose sticking out.

He couldn't tell what it was, but by walking around
to the other side he was able to reach it with a long

stick. He pulled Ann's stuffed dog out of the pond and held it, dripping, in his hands. The stomach had been ripped open, and the box that made it squeak whenever his sister hugged it was hanging by a thread.

He tried to think of an animal that might do that. A dog might have torn the toy open, but would a dog have dropped it into the pond? Maybe a muskrat had thought it was alive, but didn't they just eat trees and plants that grew around water?

It was almost dark now, and he wanted to watch a Jacques Cousteau special on TV. He hid the ripped toy dog in the bushes and went back to the house, thinking about how neat it would be to live on a boat as a professional diver. He ached to use his own tank. There'd be plenty of time after his dive to "find" the damaged puppy. He decided to use that as an excuse for disobeying his father, if he *should* need an excuse, later.

Mrs. Mason called Fred Hurlburt while the rest of the family was watching television. Mary answered, and they chatted about the children before Fred came to the phone.

"Fred? This is Olivia Mason."

"Oh, hi, Olivia. How are things? Those lively kids of yours behaving themselves?"

"Oh, we're all fine, Fred. And I hope your family

is, too." (Couldn't she just come right out and ask him?)

"Fred, we've had a little incident here at the farm." Then she told him about Ann's terror at the pond, and asked if he thought there was any danger of snakes.

"A few garter snakes grow to be quite large," he told her. "And there are a lot of harmless black snakes around. But there hasn't been anything poisonous seen around here since the Gilby boys killed a rattler five years ago. But that was up in the hills, miles from the village."

"Thank you, Fred, I feel better now. It's just that since the puppy went swimming and never came back, I've felt a little funny about that pond."

"Your puppy drowned, Olivia? I'm sorry. How are the kids taking it?"

"Oh, the baby cried for a couple of days, but she seems to be over it now. Fred, that's another thing I'm concerned about. I don't think Bingo *drowned*, but. . . ." Then she told him about hearing the yelp and the sound of splashing water. Fred was quiet on the other end.

"Fred? Are you still there?"

"Yes, Olivia, I'm still here. I was just thinking. Puppies do get lost, you know. As for little Ann, it sounds to me as if she might have scared a grand-daddy bullfrog into jumping into the water. Only she was more afraid then he."

Fred said a few words about the recent heat wave and then hung up. Mary found him staring at the floor a few minutes later, with his hand still on the receiver.

"Anything the matter over at the Masons'?"

Fred Hurlburt looked at his wife. "No," he said finally, "nothing is wrong at the Masons'. At least I hope not."

# ••• 12

Joan Ralston's mouth fell open.

"You're going where?"

"I'm going jogging. What's so strange about that?"

If Munch had told his mother he was going to the moon on a skateboard she would have found it easier to believe.

"A lot of people jog, Mom." He was wearing a pair of orange striped shorts, grown so tight they were held closed with a piece of rope. His sneakers were blue, his socks were green, and his top was an enormous yellow sweatshirt. The effect was overwhelming.

"Do you mind if I ask why you've decided to jog?" asked his mother, still staring at the boy who was usually too tired to carry his supper dishes to the sink.

"I'm sick of being the fattest kid in the world," he answered, peering out the window. "When the heck is it going to get dark?"

"You're going jogging in the dark?"

"Do you think I want anyone to see me?" he snorted.

His mother shook her head and smiled at her son. "Frederick, I think it's wonderful that you want to lose weight. I'll try to help by keeping sweets out of the house, and. . . ."

"Please, Mom," he interrupted. "It's bad enough doing this. Do we have to talk about it too?" Munch looked out the window again, then threw himself down on the sofa to wait.

He watched his mother leave the room, still shaking her head. How could he tell her that a skinny girl who recently moved in next door was the real reason he was going to risk his life tonight by jogging? He liked her. A lot. But he didn't think she liked him. Maybe it was because she called him Blubbo the flying cookie monster.

But he liked her anyway. And tonight was the beginning of the end of all the nicknames.

The cuckoo clock struck the half hour and he jumped out of his daydreams. He pulled the curtain back; it was finally dark enough. He decided to go out the back door. Then he could sneak around the house, climb over the stone wall, and walk to the road.

Wow, it was dark out there. Well, he thought, there would be street lights once he was on the road. Heaving a heavy sigh, he stepped off the porch.

And walked right into Nick Mason. The two boys yelled and tried to escape from each other — a mass of arms and legs all moving at once but getting nowhere.

"Help, Ma! I'm being kidnapped!"

Nick laughed wildly when he recognized Munch's voice. Munch started laughing too, and when his mother turned on the porch light she saw them lying in the grass holding their stomachs.

"Frederick, you said you were going jogging. What are you doing on the ground?"

Jogging! At this news Nick was rolling around again, holding his sides. But the joke was not funny to Munch, and he was serious when he got to his feet.

"Can't a guy even take a walk in his own back-yard?" He gave his mother a look to silence her. She took the hint and went inside, turning off the light, to Munch's relief. The boys went up on the porch and Munch flung himself into the hammock. So much for physical fitness night.

"So what are you doing in the clown suit, Munch, old pal? You look like a two-hundred-pound canary."

"Very funny. And do you mind telling me what you're doing, sneaking around in our yard in the middle of the night? Probably stealing tomatoes from Mom's garden."

"Stealing food is your game, not mine," Nick answered hotly. Then he laughed. "Hey, what are we fighting about? I thought we were partners in 'Mason and Ralston, Treasure Divers.' I was going to show you the plans I drew for the raft, but I think the Goon snitched the paper."

Nick stared at the large lump in the hammock and thought about the raft with that much weight on it. He bit his nails nervously.

"You still want to do it, don't you? I mean help build it and all?"

Munch glanced over at Nick. In the light from the street lamp he saw Nick chewing on his nails. "If you don't stop that," he said, "you won't be able to hold the hammer. And how can you bring up treasure with no fingers?"

Nick laughed. The raft had been his idea. On TV the divers always jumped out of a boat, but a raft would have to do. The plan was to build it and keep it hidden in the tall grass by the pond until the first opportunity they had to dive. Nick hoped he wouldn't have to wait long.

"Don't worry about me," he told Munch. "I just hope you can keep from tipping over the raft. I'll be too busy to rescue you."

Munch ignored that reference to his bulk. "There's one thing I still don't understand," he said. "Even if we do build the raft, and even if you do go to the bottom of the pond, what happens if your folks find out?"

"That's easy," Nick answered. "They don't find out. I don't tell them, you don't tell them, and my sister doesn't really know what's going on — even if she did steal the plans."

Nick stood up and stretched, yawning. "See you tomorrow, Big Bird. I've got to figure out how to get the plans for the raft back from Goon girl. Maybe I'll tie her to a tree and tickle her till she gives in." He laughed at the thought. Then he gave the hammock a push and hopped off the porch. "Good night, Frederick the Great."

Munch lay where he was and watched the night swallow up his friend. He shivered, thinking ahead to the day when the water of Shadow Pond would do the same. Finally he crawled out of the hammock.

"Frederick the Great," he muttered into the blackness of his kitchen. Another nickname to add to the collection.

## ••• 13

Gwen peered into the oven for the tenth time in as many minutes. The cake was beginning to rise, but there was a deep hole in the middle, like a dinosaur's footprint. "He won't mind," she said, smiling. "I'll just fill it with frosting."

Today was Munch's birthday, and the cake was going to match the paper on the gift she had hidden yesterday: orange and green. The inside was white until she added the food coloring. She peeked again, hoping there was enough frosting to fill the hole on the top.

Closing the oven door again, she thought about the

day her mother had taken her to the hobby store for the things she needed to make Munch's gift.

"What kind of cord will I need for macramé, please?" she had asked the man behind the counter.

The man sighed. "Missy, I got about twenty kinds here. You making a wall hanging? A pot hanger? I got to know what you plan to make before I can recommend the right cord, see?"

"Oh," she said. "For a belt. I'm making a belt for a friend."

"Well, that's more like it. Now, let's see here. I got six colors and I got three weights. You making a real nice belt, or just something sort of casual?"

Gwen swallowed. This was going to be harder than she thought. The book on macramé she had gotten from the library had made it all sound so easy. She picked out a large roll of light brown cord. "I'll take this, please."

"Is your friend a horse, missy? That's enough to make six belts. Here, take this little roll, it'll be plenty." He picked up the smallest roll on the counter.

"That's O.K., I'll just take the large." Gwen put her money down, waited for her change, and left the shop. Why was everyone so mean about fat people? Munch couldn't help it if he liked to eat.

Now, as she opened the oven for another peek, she thought about the man behind the counter again.

"You making a belt for a horse, missy?" She giggled. As it turned out, it had taken over half the roll of cord to make the belt. Of course she didn't know how big to make it, but she measured a tree trunk that looked about right and used that as a guide. The belt fit around the tree perfectly.

Her mother had agreed to let her invite Munch to dinner that night. They had worked it out so Munch's mother would come over with her gift just at the point when they lighted the candles and brought the cake in from the kitchen. The signal would be the switching off of the lights in the dining room.

To get her brother to stop teasing her had been another matter. "Munch's cake is beautiful, Sis. But what are the rest of us having for dessert?"

When that failed to get a response, Nick blew up a big yellow balloon, popped it, then in a surprisingly good imitation of Munch's voice, said, "My goodness, Gwen, I must have eaten too much of that delicious cake."

Nick got a response, but not the one he was after. Gwen was furious. How did he come off poking fun at his pal? She looked at her brother and smiled sweetly. "Nicky, I have about thirty feet of macramé cord left over. Would you like to use it on your new raft?"

"What's this?" Their father looked up from his newspaper. "Who's building a raft?"

The room was silent, until finally, Nick found his voice and started explaining how he had thought of building a raft to use on Shadow Pond, but it was just an idea.

"Be sure you keep it that way," his father said in a deadly quiet voice. "I want you kids to *stay away from that pond*. Do you hear?"

Nick nodded, his fingers crossed behind his back.

# ...14

"Hit again, harder this time." Gwen raised her arm a second time and brought it down as hard as she could. This time the bottle of coke smashed when it hit the raft. The pieces of glass stayed inside the plastic bag in which Gwen had put the bottle. "I christen you the *Gwendolyn Mason!*"

Building the raft had proved an easy matter after the boys agreed to make Gwen a third partner. With her standing guard, they were able to work without fear of being discovered by any adults. Gwen had gladly handed over the plans as soon as Nick invited her to join Project Dive.

"We might as well," Nick had told Munch. "She knows all about it anyway." Munch thought it was a good idea. He had been very pleased and flattered by

Gwen's birthday gift—and even though her cake had looked funny, it had tasted delicious. She must really like me, he decided. And he agreed with Nick that with Gwen as a partner, they wouldn't have to worry anymore. She wouldn't tell his parents that they had gone ahead with building a full-sized raft for the pond, because she was in as deep as they were.

They had gotten permission to build a raft. Only, Nick had told his father they were making a small model of a raft. No, of course they wouldn't climb on it; the model was much too small to use. Yes, of course they knew the pond was deep and probably dangerous. No, of course they wouldn't think of swimming there.

"Some model, eh, Munch, old Pal?" Nick was looking at the raft the way Washington must have surveyed his troops.

"It's beautiful, sort of." Munch was dressed as a rainbow again, but instead of rope holding up his shorts, he was wearing his brand new macramé belt.

The object of their admiration looked like a pile of boards that had been tossed together by a strong wind. And it was big — big enough to require the combined strength of all three of them to drag it into the pond, where it now lay floating.

Nick grinned at his partners. "How about that? It floats, you guys." He poked Munch in the ribs. "Just make sure you don't flip it by getting too close to the edge."

"Don't worry, I can swim," Munch said stiffly. That, in fact, was the one sport Munch could do well. His built-in flotation system and powerful arms and legs were an unsinkable combination. He'd been one of the best in his group at the "Y" in the days when he was just an average, overweight kid who could exert himself without puffing. But looking at the raft now, he was having second thoughts about his active part in Project Dive.

"What could go wrong?" Nick asked when Munch told him he was worried. "Look, it's simple. Gwen here keeps watch while you and I paddle out to the middle. Then after I descend, you just wait till I come up again."

Nick looked hard at Munch's troubled face. "Of course, if you'd rather be the look-out, I'll ask my sister to be my crew."

Munch was silent, making his decision. "O.K., but on one condition. We tie a rope around your waist. In case anything goes wrong, at least we can drag your body up."

Nick laughed, but it sounded forced to Munch's and Gwen's ears. "Have it your way," he said. "Now let's cover this thing with weeds and get out of here."

So the plan was still go. All three had jobs to do before the launching could take place. Nick was to assemble his equipment and hide it all in one place. Munch was supposed to find some strong rope and "borrow" his father's canoe paddles.

Gwen's job was the hardest. She had to find out when her mother was going shopping, then invent enough errands to keep her away until the diving operation was completed.

Deep down, in the bottom of the pond, the thing that lived there was hungry all the time now. How many lights and darks had passed since it had caught the fast-swimming muskrat? And one paddling creature too, but that had been so small. Now it felt a constant aching emptiness inside.

Almost a century of living had taught the thing to seize whatever it could for food. For a long time now there had only been tiny fish and tadpoles, and they were nearly gone. Perhaps the time had come to leave. But something—the activity at the edge of the pond, perhaps — kept it hidden here, waiting.

Now, at last, something was happening on the surface, near the light. Vibrations, movement. That usually meant a swimming creature had entered the water.

The shadowy thing left its cave and started the rise through layers of water. Its small, ancient eyes could see only a short distance. But the wrinkled skin around the ears could detect the faintest vibrations. As it felt them now, its stomach began to secrete the juices that would soon digest whatever was up above.

The thing paused in its upward rise. Danger! Something had thundered into the water. Now the pond was agitated, a mass of vibrations. Quickly the thing lowered itself to the bottom again to wait.

Gradually, the vibrations grew smaller and smaller, then nothing.

The thing still waited. Then, when all seemed still, it rose slowly, ponderous in its great size. On the surface, a large, dark thing floated, blocking out the light. It lay motionless, unbreathing. The water was still. The Shadow moved under the raft and touched whatever had entered the water. This was not food; it was hard, like the logs on the bottom of the pond.

Bewildered, angry, hungry, the Shadow floated toward the bottom. It swam back into the cave, waiting for food to enter the water.

# ● ● ● 15

Mrs. Mason shook the thermometer down and placed it under Gwen's tongue, despite her daughter's protest that all she had was a headache.

"I just want to stay in my room where it's a little cooler," Gwen had told her mother when she proposed they make a shopping trip to Hartford.

"That's O.K., we'll go tomorrow instead, when you're feeling better. I'll put off my errands and get a few groceries here in the village."

Ever since Ann's scare, Mrs. Mason had not wanted to leave any of the children home alone. She had begun to share her husband's uneasiness about the pond, though she felt foolish about it. All the children, even Annie, knew how to swim. But

Gwen's headache seemed a good excuse to stay home.

Gwen realized she had to do some fast talking, or all their plans would be ruined. She quickly pulled the thermometer out of her mouth. "But, Mom," she said, "my pictures are ready and I'm dying to see them. Besides, Annie will be disappointed if you don't go. I'll be O.K., honest."

Olivia looked at her daughter thoughtfully and felt her forehead. "Well, all right. You don't seem really ill. I'll just call Joan Ralston and ask her to keep an eye on you two. I won't stay long in Hartford. Now promise me you won't fight with your brother."

That had become an unnecessary request, Mrs. Mason realized suddenly. Gwen and Nick had had their heads together every minute for the past week. She hoped they weren't up to some mischief, but it certainly was a relief not to hear the bickering that had gone on between them for nearly ten years. Perhaps they were growing up at last.

"Mom, before you go, would you ask Nick if I can borrow a few of his comics?" Gwen had to let Nick know that today was the day.

Her mother had been straightening up her room. Closing the drawers. Opening the windows. Smoothing the blankets. Now she stopped and said mildly, "You really shouldn't read if you have a headache, Gwen."

(Oh great.) "I'll just look at the pictures. O.K.?"

Her mother poked her head into Nick's room. "Your sister isn't feeling well, Nick. Would you mind letting her look at your comics? She'll be careful with them."

Nick knew what "careful" meant to his baby sister. He'd had to throw away a lot of comics that she'd been "careful with" in the past. "Oh, Mom, can't you get Annie some of her own comics? She wrecks mine in about two minutes."

"Not Annie, silly. It's Gwen who wants to borrow them. She has a headache and doesn't want to go shopping with us. She just wants something to read, that's all."

Nick froze. He'd gotten the message. "Where are you going?" He tried not to sound too interested.

"I'm taking Annie to Hartford to get some shoes. She's practically walking out of those old brown ones. And your father needs a few things. Want to come along?"

Ordinarily Nick would have, and he knew his mother knew it. He decided to play it cool. "I'd like to, Mom. But I'm right in the middle of something. Thanks, anyway. When are you coming back?"

"I won't be too long, with your sister not feeling well. Besides, it'll be pretty hot in Hartford. We should be back maybe around lunchtime."

Nick figured that would be enough time for their dive. But with his luck he'd probably still be on the bottom when she came driving into the yard. How could he delay her? More errands, of course! "Say Mom, could you get me a couple of things in Hartford?" (Quick! What did he need?)

"Of course. What do you want? How about some new T-shirts? And those cut-offs should be thrown away."

"Sure, that would be great." Ordinarily, Nick would never have agreed to wear ready-made shorts. But he was willing to sacrifice his two-year-old cut-off jeans for some extra time.

"And some more tube socks for basketball. And some underwear. O.K.?"

"Maybe you should come with me to try on some of these things. You've grown a lot this summer."

"Taller, not fatter. I'm no Munch, Mom." They both laughed and his mother went to get Ann ready for the trip. Nick grabbed a handful of comics and crashed through Gwen's door.

"Get up! It's Dive Day!"

# ···16

Joan Ralston was in the pantry kneading bread when she heard the knock on the kitchen door. "Can you get that, Frederick? My hands are doughy."

Munch opened the door and let in two very excited Masons. "She's gone. Hurry up!"

Mrs. Ralston came out of the pantry at that moment, so they tried to act as if it was a perfectly normal summer morning.

"Who's gone?" she asked.

"My mother. She's gone to Hartford, to shop." Gwen found her voice first.

"Oh, I know that. Your mother called a few minutes ago to ask if I'd see that you two don't get into any mischief while she's gone. How's your headache, Gwen?"

Gwen swallowed. Twice. "Fine. I mean I feel better, thank you."

"Frederick, can you close your mouth?" Munch's mouth had fallen open when Gwen and Nick had first come into the kitchen. Now he snapped it shut, grinning sheepishly.

"Would you like some orange juice? Frederick was just having his breakfast."

Nick answered for both of them. "No, thank you. We'll just wait by the p——— hammock. Come on, Gwen."

Munch finally managed to speak. "I'm not really hungry, Mom. I'll just go out now, I guess."

"You'll go nowhere until you've had your breakfast. You're still growing, you know."

Nick and Gwen went out to the porch. "You wait here, Sis. I'll go get the tank and stuff. Tell Munch to bring the rope and not to forget his watch."

Gwen watched her brother leap over the stone wall and disappear around the side of the barn. Why were her hands sweating? She knew why, of course. What they were planning to do was not only forbidden; it was dangerous. Ever since they had slid the raft into the pond and covered it with weeds, her heart had been playing tricks. What if something did happen to her brother? What if...?

"Whurf Nock?" Munch was still stuffing toast in his mouth when he came out of the house.

Gwen didn't answer his question, so he swallowed and tried again. "Where's Nick?"

"Gone to get the you-know-what. He wants you to get what you were supposed to get and don't forget your Mickey Mouse."

"What?" Munch was still not sure that what was happening was really *it*. Gwen grabbed his arm and yanked him off the porch. When they were far enough from the house she told him that Nick had gone for the tank and that he was supposed to get the other things.

"You mean it's really today?" At least six times during the last three days Munch had started to walk over to his friend's house to tell him it was no deal. He couldn't do it though. If he refused to keep watch on the raft, the name-calling would never end. And he would lose a friend. He might lose him anyway, but that was something he was definitely not going to think about.

"Yes, silly. Mom's gone shopping and it's all set. We've given her a long list of errands, so she shouldn't be back for hours."

"Hey, you two. What's all the whispering?" Mrs. Ralston had come up behind them, and they hadn't heard her sneakers on the grass. She was carrying her garden things.

"Mom, what're you doing?"

"I'm going to do a little weeding before the sun gets around. Why?"

Munch stared at his mother. Gwen stared at Munch. Mrs. Ralston shook her head. Had the heat affected all the children today?

"Let me do it, Mom."

"Can I do it for you, Mrs. Ralston? I love to garden."

Both Gwen and Munch realized that if she stayed in the backyard they'd have to scrap the plan for today. Nick would soon be coming back with the tank!

Joan Ralston laughed. "When my son offers to pull weeds, how can I refuse? And Gwen, don't you go getting another headache." Finally she handed over the gardening basket.

"And when you're finished, Frederick Everett Ralston, I think you'd better see Dr. Melvin for a check-up. You haven't been your lazy self for a week!"

She was laughing as she walked away. Of course she knew the kids were up to some mischief, but that's what kids were all about, wasn't it? She'd get busy cleaning those shelves in the basement where she planned to put her jars of canned fruits and vegetables. Later she'd check on Frederick and Gwen. They'd probably welcome some lemonade after their work.

Gwen looked at Munch. "That was close. And here comes Nick."

They watched him lope across the yard as if he didn't have any idea they'd been waiting for him.

"Hi. What's happening?" They told him how they had gotten Mrs. Ralston to go inside by volunteering to do her weeding.

"That's great. Gwen stays here in the garden. That way she can keep her eyes on both houses. No sweat."

The three looked at each other, not quite believing what was about to happen. Nick spoke first. "Well? Do we stand here all day? Come on, Munch, let's get going."

# ...17

Olivia Mason glanced at the speedometer and let up on the gas pedal. Why was she driving so fast? The children were certainly old enough to be alone for three hours, and Joan was right next door. She relaxed and smiled at her youngest daughter sitting beside her.

"I know someone who is getting new shoes today," she said.

"Red. I want red shoes."

"Red? Well, we'll have to see if they have any red shoes today."

She parked in the ramp garage near a big department store. Most of her errands could be done there, then she'd have to walk a couple of blocks to pick up Gwen's film. No. She'd do that first, since it was already getting warm. She'd get the pictures, then have coffee while Annie ate some ice cream, and then she'd tackle the list in her purse.

The air-conditioning in the photo shop felt lovely after the heat of the streets. "Hello. My daughter has some pictures being developed here."

She handed the claim stub to the clerk, who went into another room, then returned in a few minutes to say, "I'm sorry, but they don't seem to be in yet."

"But they were supposed to be here yesterday." Olivia Mason felt annoyed. Would she have to drive back later in the week?

"Today's shipment hasn't yet arrived. Can you come back in about forty-five minutes, after the mail comes?"

"Yes, I guess I can. Tell me, is there any place near here where I can get some ice cream for my little girl?"

By the time Mrs. Mason had had two cups of coffee, wiped chocolate ice cream off little Ann's face and hands, and walked back to the photography shop, it was almost eleven o'clock.

The pictures had come in. "Here they are, Mrs. Mason. That will be $3.67, please."

Relieved, Olivia paid and put the envelope of pictures in her purse. At the same time she took out the shopping list and glanced at it. She took her daughter's hand. "Come on, Honey. Mommy has a lot to do."

## ● ● ● 18

The water was warmer than Nick thought it would be. He was hanging onto the side of the raft while adjusting his mask with his free hand. The raft was in the middle of the pond. They had maneuvered it there easily, each using a canoe paddle. The raft floated nicely, even with both boys on it.

They couldn't see Gwen from the pond because the barn was in the way. But she promised to check on them every few minutes. If they needed anything, Munch would let her know and she would get it. It was a perfect plan.

"Is the rope O.K.?" Munch watched as Nick tied it

around his waist; then he tied the other end around his own. "This way you can yank when you want to come up, and I'll be able to feel it."

It had been Munch's suggestion. Munch could not explain, even to himself, why he felt this was so necessary. But it made him feel better, as he watched his friend jump off the raft, to know he was tied to him.

Nick stuck his face in the water to de-fog his mask. The rope was securely tied, the tank felt good, and the oxygen was turned on. He was ready. Except for the watch that Dumbo had forgotten.

"What do you mean, you forgot it?" Nick had yelled. "How will I know when my time is up?"

"I just didn't put it on this morning. Then when you guys came crashing through the door, it completely slipped my mind. I'm really sorry, Nick."

Nick squinted into the sun. "I'll just stay down about a half hour, and I have oxygen enough for almost twice that. No sweat." He looked up at Munch, kneeling near the edge of the raft. "Give me a good yank after about a half hour. O.K.?"

"How am I supposed to know when a half hour is up without a watch?" Munch asked.

"Weren't you ever in the scouts? Check the sun. When it's right over your head it'll be noon. It must be about ten-thirty now. At eleven it'll be just coming over the roof of the barn. Got it?"

"Yeah, I guess so."

"Good. Well, so long, old pal."

Suddenly there were only bubbles where Nick's face had been. Munch's heart was pounding and he felt a little sick. Check the sun. He looked up and was blinded. How could the sun help him keep track of the time if he couldn't even look at it?

Below, Nick stared into the brown gloom beneath the surface of the pond. His heart was beating fast too. The book said to relax and breathe slowly. He tried it and he felt better.

He looked up. The silhouette of the raft was still visible. He looked down. Nothing but darkness. He threw his arms over his head, forcing his body to move toward the bottom. And then his feet touched something. Yuck. His flippers were buried in weeds and mud. He began swimming then, more to get out of those weeds than anything else.

He hadn't counted on its being so dark. He could see maybe fifteen feet around him, no more. The rest was a murky unknown. He stopped swimming to check the rope. There was still plenty left. He was secretly glad Munch had thought of it. At least he was tied to something up there.

He put his feet down again. More mud, but then his right foot struck something hard. He peered down. A huge, flat rock was just under him. There were no weeds here. He flicked his feet and he was upside down, groping for a hand-hold on the rock. That was easy, because the rock was flat, like a shelf.

Pulling, he positioned himself next to the rock where it curved outward from the mud. He couldn't believe his eyes. Under the rock the mud had been scooped out and he was staring into a small, under-water cave!

# •••19

Olivia Mason and Joan Ralston were both sitting
down, resting with their shoes off. Joan was in her
basement where she had been working. She had finished the shelves and was taking a few minutes' break
before carrying the dusty jars over to the sink to wash
them.

Olivia Mason was sitting under a tree in front of
the Hartford Public Library. Ann was tired and this
was a good spot to stop. Olivia leaned against the tree
and closed her eyes, only half listening to the traffic
on Main Street.

"Mommy, I want gum." Ann had also removed her
shoes and was imitating her mother, back against the
tree, legs swinging free under the bench.

When Olivia opened her purse to take out a stick of gum, she noticed the envelope containing Gwen's pictures. Curious to see what Gwen had snapped, she began looking through the glossy prints. The house, a bit out of focus. Then a picture of herself, bending over in her garden. Wait till I get my hands on that little sneak, she smiled.

And then there it was. She had to look closely before the fact of what her eyes were seeing registered in her brain. Standing in a dark room were two boys. The fat one was Munch Ralston. His arms were blurred as if he had moved them just as the picture was taken. The other boy was Nick, her son. His mouth was fuzzy, as if he had been talking when the camera clicked.

But the thing that caught Olivia Mason's attention was what Nick had on his back. *That* wasn't blurred, it was very clear. *He was wearing an oxygen tank for scuba diving.*

Olivia felt cold, even though the air around her was over eighty degrees. She saw it all clearly now: Gwen's headache, Nick's various requests that would delay her return. . . .

It was a plan, the whole thing had been a plan! Now she understood why Nick and Gwen had been spending so much time together. All that whispering at night after they thought she and Barry were asleep. There was only one place where Nick would use an oxygen tank.

Angry and yet sick with dread, she pushed Ann's small feet into her shoes, stepped into her own, picked up the child, and rushed toward the garage.

The attendant looked up to see the pale face of a frantic woman in front of his window.

"A telephone, I need a telephone quickly. My son is in trouble, please."

"This is a garage, lady. No phone here. You got to go across the street to the store. That's the closest." He looked at the small child standing next to the strange lady who was pulling things out of her purse. The child didn't look like he was in trouble. He didn't even look like a boy.

"Please, can you give me change?" The attendant took the dollar bill, made change, then watched as Olivia Mason crossed one of the busiest intersections in Hartford. Against the light.

She found a phone near the entrance of the store. "Stay right here," she commanded Ann, and stepped into the booth. It was sweltering. She'd call her husband's office first, then Joan Ralston. No. If she were all wrong, why upset Barry? She dialed the Ralston number.

"Please don't be busy," she begged. The line wasn't busy but the phone rang and rang. Joan, in her basement, was washing the canning jars. With the water running, she couldn't hear the phone ringing upstairs.

Olivia Mason was near tears. She dug her dime out

of the slot and shoved it back into the telephone. Then she dialed her husband's office.

"Simpson, Welch and Barrett — may I help you?" The receptionist's cheery voice did little to calm her.

"This is Mrs. Barry Mason. Is my husband free to speak to me? It's very important."

"One moment, Mrs. Mason. I'll ring him." It seemed forever before she heard Barry's voice.

"Hello? Honey? What's wrong? The operator said it. . . ."

"Barry, it's Nick. I think he's done something stupid." She told him about Gwen's "headache," Nick's delaying action of requests for new clothing, and finally, painfully, she described the picture she'd seen of Nick wearing the tank. Barry didn't say anything for a minute. Then he told his wife to hurry home. He'd make some calls of his own, meanwhile.

Olivia Mason opened the door of the booth, took her surprised little girl by the arm, and hurried across to the garage. In spite of Hartford's lunch hour traffic, she drove like a race-car driver back toward home — and the pond.

# ... 20

Now that he was really at the bottom of the pond, Nick was disappointed. The "cave" turned out to be no more than the underside of the great, jutting rock that came out of the mud at an angle, like a roof. It was deep, though, and when he went in he found that his feet went further back than he had expected.

He gazed out from under the rock's overhang and wondered how long he'd been down. Ten or fifteen minutes at the most. No sweat. He still had plenty of time to explore before Munch's yank would tell him that half an hour had gone by. Under the rock, the bottom was smooth, almost as if it had been swept. There were no plants nor the rotten debris of leaves and logs that he'd found elsewhere on the bottom.

Nick traced the rope back with his eye. It was

pulled taut by the overhanging rock. Then it disappeared in the darkness of the water. He had just decided he wasn't going to spend his last fifteen minutes under a rock pretending he had discovered treasure, and had started to swim out, when he thought he saw something move in the water ahead of him.

It wasn't a fast movement like a fish's, but more as if the shadows and weeds on the bottom had changed their shape. He stopped, stared, and waited. His eyes tried to pierce through the gloom to find some shape in what he had just seen, or thought he had seen. He saw weeds, one or two fallen trees, their branches covered with slime and rotted leaves, and a few large rocks. But nothing that could move.

And then he saw movement again. This time he was sure. The "rocks" he had been staring at had changed shape, gotten bigger. Nick's heart slammed against his ribs and he felt numbed with fear. Something out there was moving toward him slowly, steadily — something huge.

Nick gave himself three fast commands without taking time to think: 1) don't try to swim for the surface; 2) stay put until that thing reveals itself or goes away; 3) let Munch know I'm in trouble, fast!

Backing under the rock as far as he could go, Nick began pulling the safety rope in with him. It was longer than he remembered, but finally he felt it pull tight. He gave a few quick tugs, stopped, waited. That ought to alert Munch, he thought. But pulling the rope into the cave had muddied the water around him so that he could no longer see out of the cave as he waited.

In the darkness, the Shadow waited too, for there was something in its lair. Every instinct warned it to attack whatever was trying to take over its cave. It moved forward, jaws open and ready. Something had stirred up the bottom, muddying the water. But years in this place had taught it to recognize every weed, every pebble. It stopped again. When it could see, it would enter the cave and destroy whatever was there.

Now Nick could not seem to get enough oxygen. He felt dizzy, light-headed, wanting to giggle. But the water had cleared enough for him to see out of the cave again. And what he saw nearly caused him to spit out the mouthpiece and scream for help. For there, in front of the rock, gripping the bottom with claws like a bear, was an *enormous* snapping turtle. The back was covered with green slime, and the head, on a neck as thick as a baseball bat, waved back and forth less than six feet from Nick's face. The last thing he noticed was the pink throat that was revealed as the jaws opened.

"It's as big around as Munch." This was Nick Mason's last thought before he lost consciousness.

## ••• 21

"... fifty-eight, (one thousand); fifty-nine, (one thousand); sixty." Munch Ralston was counting seconds. In one minute he would give the first tug on the rope. This would tell Nick that the time was up and that he should surface. But he didn't really know how much time had passed since he had watched Nick slide under the water. If only he hadn't forgotten his watch.

Terrified that maybe too much time had gone by, he gave a sharp yank on the rope. Several feet of it landed at his feet. He pulled again and again. Finally he felt resistance at the other end. He waited for Nick's answering tug. Nothing came, and at that instant Munch knew something was wrong.

He began pulling on the rope, hoping that, whatever was going on down there, Nick would come swimming to the surface, safe and smiling. But even if Nick had been conscious, he wouldn't have felt Munch's tug on the rope. It was tangled in the branch of a dead tree, five feet from where the turtle kept watch over the trespasser in its den.

The instinct that said "attack" was checked by the size of the intruder, still in the cave. Never before had the turtle confronted something larger than itself. Now it was confused. Suddenly there was movement above it in the water. It turned to face the new danger.

Munch didn't know when he decided he was going into the water. All he knew was that he must, and that seconds counted. Holding a deep breath, he jumped off the raft and began pulling himself along the rope toward whatever was holding Nick on the bottom.

The tree branch was in front of him before he knew it. While he was working on the tangle, something moved at the edge of his vision. Holding onto the branch to anchor himself, he peered into the gloom. And his blood seemed to stop. Sitting at the edge of a flat rock with the rope passing under its body, was a turtle so big it was like a nightmare. A gigantic, mean, snapping turtle.

Munch saw what he had to do, and hoped there would be time. He broke the branch that held the rope, then, turning, forced himself toward the surface. With one hand he grabbed a canoe paddle, and pushing himself away from the raft with the other hand, did a perfect turn-around.

He went down slower this time, unable to use the rope to pull himself along. He held the paddle like a spear, using his legs and free arm to propel himself.

The turtle had his back to him. Without thinking of the consequences, he jabbed at the broad back with the handle of the paddle. The turtle flipped over, its head striking like a snake's, as its massive jaws clamped onto the paddle. The turtle shook the paddle as if it were a straw, claws tearing at this new enemy.

Munch swam past, reached into the cave, and felt his hand touch something. All in the same second, he grabbed, pulled, and began kicking for the surface. When his brain stopped helping him, momentum carried him up.

He was clutching a limp thing that twenty minutes earlier had been his friend, Nick Mason.

Annoyed at having to pull weeds all alone, Gwen disobeyed her orders. After ten minutes of pretending, she walked to the corner of the barn and sat in the grass. She had a clear view of Munch on the raft, but the tall weeds kept him from seeing her.

She didn't mean to doze, but the sun made her sleepy and the wood felt warm as she leaned against the barn. When she looked again she had to blink to make sure. The raft was there, floating serenely in the still water. But Munch was not on it. He was nowhere in sight. She jumped up, ran to the edge of the pond and screamed. "Munch! Where are you?" Then she turned and ran as fast as she could toward the house. Mrs. Ralston was just coming up the cellar stairs when Gwen burst through the kitchen door.

"Gwen, what's wrong? You look...."

"Come quick! Nick's gone to the bottom of the pond and Munch is supposed to be on the raft only he's gone too and I don't know what's wrong, please..."

She never finished because her own mother flew into the kitchen at that minute. "Joan, where's Nick?"

For a second, the three stared at each other. Then Gwen's stricken face sent both women running after her toward the pond. Little Ann was still in the car, fast asleep.

Joan Ralston screamed when she saw her son's body break the surface. But he was gone again before he heard her voice, or the shriek of the police car and ambulance roaring across the backyard.

# ● ● ● 22

They were all there when Nick opened his eyes. If he'd had the strength, he would have laughed at their white faces staring at him like a family of owls.

"What's happening?" His words seemed to come from a long tunnel.

"What's happening, young man," said a strange voice, "is that you're lucky to be able to ask that question." It was a man wearing a white suit. In fact, everything was white: the ceiling, the curtain around his bed, the sheet covering him.

Then Nick remembered. The raft, the water, the cave under the rock. And the turtle. Then nothing, until he had opened his eyes and seen his family around him.

"Where's Munch?" he asked suddenly. The doctor pulled the curtain away from the right side of Nick's bed. On another bed, a few feet away, Munch lay covered to the neck by a sheet.

"He's going to be fine, Nick," the doctor said. Then Nick heard the story, first from Gwen, then his mother, and finally his father: how his mother had seen Gwen's picture of the tank, how his father had called the police from his office, how Munch had floated to the surface with Nick in his arms.

"We'd like to hear your part of it, Nick, when you feel more like talking." It was his father.

His part of it made Nick feel like crawling back under the rock and staying there. He had scared his mother to death, he'd gotten Gwen mixed up in dangerous business. And Munch, who had saved his life, might have drowned because of him. He himself might have drowned. He wanted to tell his father how he felt, but he couldn't.

"I just don't feel like talking right now, Dad. I'm sorry about everything."

Barry smiled. "It's O.K., Nick, I've got a few things to be sorry for myself. Get well so I can tell you about them."

Nick's eyes blurred. He turned to look at Munch in the other bed.

"Don't worry about him," the doctor said. "He swallowed about half that pond getting you up, and we had to pump him out. When the sedative wears off you two will be trading lies again. Now you get some rest before I send you home."

Then Nick was alone in the room except for the mound in the next bed. "Not lies," he said to himself. "You don't tell lies to your best friend."

## EPILOGUE

The three children stared into the aquarium. It took up almost a whole wall of the reptile room in the Roaring Brook Nature Center.

The filter system gurgled, but there was no other sound. On the bottom, the turtle sat still except for the swaying motion of its head. It, too, seemed to be staring.

Gwen spoke first. "Won't he die in this tank after living in the pond for so long?"

"The man said they'd feed him regularly here. If he'd stayed in the pond he wouldn't have lived another year," Munch answered. "There was just no food left."

"Mr. Hurlburt says now that he's out of the pond we can stock it with fish again." Nick added, "He says that turtle has probably been in there for years and years. The old man who owned our place knew about it, he says, and tried to protect the kids who wanted to swim there. And everyone thought he was being mean."

"Can we leave now?" Gwen asked. "That turtle gives me the creeps."

"Yeah, me too," said Munch, who looked a lot thinner than he had a few weeks ago.

As they walked toward the exit, a pair of ancient eyes turned and watched them until they became a blur. Then the Shadow turned its eyes back to the surface of the tank to wait for the ripples that meant food.